CREEPY CREATURES

SNAKE SHOCK

Collect all the

CREEPY CREATURES

SNAKE SHOCK

SPIDER FRIGHT

BAT ATTACK

RAT PANIC

TOAD TERROR

CREEPY CREATURES

SNAKE SHOCK

ED GRAVES

SCHOLASTIC

First published in the UK in 2010 by Scholastic Children's Books
An imprint of Scholastic Ltd
Euston House, 24 Eversholt Street
London, NW1 1DB, UK
Registered office: Westfield Road, Southam, Warwickshire, CV47 0RA
SCHOLASTIC and associated logos are trademarks and/or registered
trademarks of Scholastic Inc.
Series created by Working Partners Ltd

Text copyright © Working Partners Ltd, 2010
The right of Ed Graves to be identified as the author of this work
has been asserted by him.

ISBN 978 1407 11715 7

Printed in the UK by CPI Bookmarque, Croydon, Surrey.
Papers used by Scholastic Children's Books are made
from wood grown in sustainable forests.

1 3 5 7 9 10 8 6 4 2

www.scholastic.co.uk/zone

With special thanks to Tracey Turner

For Jamie Morgan, who first thought of the idea when each day we walked past an old lady's garden full of stone animals and gnomes, and imagined them all coming to life at night.

This Book Belongs To

— — — — — — — — — — — —

Beware!

Never open my Book, unless you

want the Curse of Gnome upon you.

Or is it too late?

Then my creatures will terrify

and torment you.

You can't imagine how scared you will be.

Gnome Gardens belongs to me.

Only me. You shall see. . .

CHAPTER ONE

Gnome Gardens

A bat swooped towards Jamie. He staggered away, only to come face to face with a snake, its jaws gaping.

"Get away from me!" he cried, imagining the snake's hiss. But – nothing. The snake was frozen, its polished scales glistening. Glancing around, Jamie saw rats, toads, spiders – even a vicious-looking wolf's snarling face. He couldn't help shuddering. *They look alive!* he thought. If he squinted at the wooden carvings, he could almost believe he was in the middle of a wild forest, about to be attacked. He took a step backwards – and tripped over a toy car, sprawling on the bedroom floor.

"You and your stupid cars, Harry!" said Jamie.

Jamie and his younger brother, Harry, had just moved into their new home, Gnome Gardens, deep in the countryside. Granddad had left the ancient house to their mum and dad. It was nothing like the squashed flat they'd lived in before, back in the city. It was enormous – three storeys high – and topped with turrets and scowling gargoyles.

Huge fireplaces gaped in each room and draughts blew through the corridors, making the doors creak on their hinges.

Jamie brushed away an enormous cobweb that dangled from the high ceiling almost to the floorboards. "There must be some giant spiders in this house, Harry," he told his brother, wiggling his fingers at him.

"Urrggh!" Harry pushed Jamie away. "Don't say that!" His voice echoed in the big, empty room. "Look at this," he said. There was a carved nest of wide-beaked baby birds on the windowsill. One of them seemed about to take flight. Jamie noticed a hawk carved into the top of the window frame, poised to swoop down on the helpless chick, its beak and talons looking sharp and deadly.

Harry turned to pick through an unpacked box. "Not *more* copies of the *Book of Gnome!*" He held up four versions of the same old-fashioned paperback. Granddad had been a writer, and *The Book of Gnome* was his best-seller. Their mum sometimes talked about the original copy, lost long ago.

Jamie groaned. "Let's just leave them in the box," he said. "Who'd want to read about stupid garden gnomes anyway?"

There was a sound at the door and Mum came into the room with two glasses of juice. She looked round at the full boxes and suitcases, her eyebrows raised. "I see you've got a lot done, then," she said, handing them the glasses. She ruffled Harry's untidy mop of dark brown hair, and he rolled his eyes at Jamie.

Jamie tried not to laugh. Harry was the youngest by two years, and Mum was always fussing over him.

"It's all right," said Mum. "I know it's exciting. Think of the adventures you'll have in this lovely old house. Imagine all the wooden creatures coming to life."

"Mum? I'm nine – too old for make-believe!" Jamie said. Secretly, he loved imagining things, but he didn't like to admit it.

"Did Granddad do all the carvings?" asked Harry, gazing intently at a little wooden beetle. He was probably trying to work out how Granddad had carved it; Harry always loved to know how things were done.

"I think so." Mum looked at Jamie. "If

you're bored with unpacking, why don't you go outside and explore the garden?"

Jamie and Harry grinned at each other, drained their glasses and charged out of the room.

"Don't get lost, or fall down wells, or get eaten by wild animals!" Mum called after them.

"We won't!" Jamie called back, laughing. But he wondered what might be lurking outside this strange house.

The two boys pounded down the staircase, across the echoing hall, and hurtled along a dark corridor to one of the back doors of the house.

Jamie opened the door and gave a gasp as they stepped into the garden. It was a wilderness of twisted branches and long grass. Gnome Gardens sat high on a hill, the enormous tangle of greenery falling away to the purple distance. Jamie stared round at the overgrown trees and bushes, crumbling statues and birdbaths. There were patches of weeds that might once have been flower beds. How had the garden become so wild?

Harry was grinning beside him. "Come on!" Jamie yelled, and they ran down the hill, trampling through the waist-high grass. They scrambled past thorny bushes and creepers that grew all the way back up to the house, completely covering some of its windows.

"Creepy!" said Harry, pointing at a bare, pale tree ripped in two by lightning. Thick honeysuckle covered its trunk, as if it were trying to throttle it. They climbed over a low wall into a long-abandoned vegetable garden, where an ancient greenhouse tottered in the corner.

"Ow!" muttered Jamie, untangling a bramble that had snagged his sleeve. When he peeled it away, his hand was covered in tiny red scratches.

"Look, Jamie!" Harry was pointing at something on the other side of some old apple trees. "What's that?"

It looked like a heap of old grey stones.

"Come on." Jamie grinned at his brother. "Let's go and find out!"

They made their way through the orchard, tripping over roots, ducking cobwebs and avoiding the fat brown slugs that slithered everywhere.

"It's a well!" said Jamie, as they came

closer. It was big and crumbling, and leaned dangerously to one side. A rusty iron handle operated an even rustier chain. The roof had shed some of its black tiles, which lay smashed on the ground. Jamie peered down the shaft at a reflection of the sky and an ancient bucket. He felt shapes underneath his fingers on the rim of the well and saw that stone snakes slithered around it, coiling over one another.

"How does it work?" Harry rattled the chain, and the sudden jangling noise made Jamie jump. A piece of rust plopped into the water below.

Swish, swish, rustled the long grasses at the other side of the well. Jamie grabbed Harry's arm.

"What—?" began Harry.

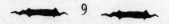

"Shhhh! Listen!" Jamie whispered.

Someone – or something – was coming towards them. It sounded as if it were dragging a heavy object behind it. Jamie and Harry looked at each other.

"Let's go and investigate," Jamie whispered. He was already imagining what might be out there. A monster? More snakes?

Harry's eyes were wide. "Didn't Mum say something about wild animals?" he asked, his voice trembling.

Jamie's heart beat loudly in his chest as they crept through the apple trees. The thing was on the other side of a hawthorn bush now, crashing through the grass. He grabbed Harry's arm and pulled him down among the thorny undergrowth. "Hide!"

CHAPTER TWO

The Secret Curse

The bush rustled. Branches parted. . .

"It's a girl!" Harry whispered. She emerged from the undergrowth, dragging branches and creepers and humming to herself.

"What's she doing with those bits of tree?" Harry murmured. The girl was thin, and the branches looked heavy, but she dragged them easily to the well. She arranged the biggest ones around the base, tucking in thorny twigs and creepers. She caught her finger on one of the sharp spines and wiped the blood on her jeans.

"Hey!" Jamie called. "Who are you? What are you doing in our garden?"

The girl spun around, dropping some of the ivy. As the boys stepped out of their hiding place, she stopped humming and frowned. Then she turned away and carried on knotting a trail of ivy together.

Jamie and Harry looked at one another. Was she ignoring them?

"What are you doing?" Jamie asked again, slightly louder.

"Making a display, what does it look like?" She added a branch of holly to the others around the base of the well. Her display was full of prickles and sharp thorns, snaking ivy and dark berries.

"But what's it for?" asked Harry.

The girl rolled her eyes. "Doesn't anyone round here know *anything*?" she said. "My library books say that you can make a special display around wells to keep bad things away." She propped a rotting turnip against the branches. "I'm going round all the wells in the village making displays."

Jamie tried not to smile. She didn't really believe that, did she?

"I'm Jamie and this is Harry," he said. "We've just moved into Gnome Gardens."

"I know. You're from the city." The girl smiled at last. "I'm Milly. I live there." She pointed down the hill to a black-tiled roof.

"It's called Gardener's Cottage, because that's what it used to be."

Harry was poking at Milly's display with a twig, trying to work out how she'd put it together. "Whoops!" A thorny branch fell to the ground.

Milly dived to scoop it up. "Careful! I've used all the most powerful plants here – thorns, and ivy." She pointed to a branch covered with shiny black berries. "The display's got to be strong enough to keep away the Gnome."

Jamie caught Harry's eye. "Are you trying to say there are garden gnomes waiting to leap out and attack us?" he asked Milly.

"Not garden gnomes. A Gnome," said Milly. She rolled her eyes again. "So you haven't even heard of the Curse of the Gnome?"

"Er, no," Jamie said, smiling.

"Look," Milly sighed, "I'll explain this slowly, since you're from the city. The Gnome is powerful. You wouldn't want to meet him, I'm telling you. And *you* should especially look out, considering where you live." She pointed at the grey-stone house squatting at the top of the hill.

Gnome Gardens. The smile faded from Jamie's face. A cool breeze curled round him and he felt the hairs on the back of his neck stand up.

"Just be careful up there. Watch out for the Gnome." Milly walked over to a rose bush covered in vicious-looking thorns. She began cutting down the spikiest branches with a pair of gardening scissors.

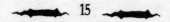

"But you don't really believe in all this, do you?" said Jamie.

"I read about it," Milly said. "It's an old, old story, the Curse of the Gnome. He'll come back to claim his land. And when he does . . . you'd better watch out."

"Well, I don't believe a word of it, but we'll give you a hand if you like." As Jamie picked up a handful of thorny twigs, he felt that cool breeze again. He shivered.

"Maybe you do believe it, then. Just a little bit," said Milly, smiling.

"No, we don't!" Harry protested, pulling strips of creeper from the apple trees. "Our granddad wrote a book about a Gnome, you know. But that was about a million years ago. We're not scared of some gnome."

"Why don't you prove it, then?" said Milly.

"How about we meet here at midnight? Of course, if you're too scared. . ."

"OK," said Jamie, folding his arms. "We'll show—"

Harry was tugging on his sleeve. "Anything could happen at *midnight*," he said. "There might be wild animals out here, or ghosts, or something even worse."

"I knew you'd be too chicken," said Milly.

"If we don't meet her, we'll never hear the end of it," Jamie whispered to Harry. "It's just a stupid story about a garden gnome. Nothing's going to happen to us."

Harry hesitated. *Oh, come on*, Jamie willed him. Eventually, his brother gave a reluctant nod.

"You're on!" said Jamie to Milly.

Milly grinned at them, then snatched up her gardening scissors and slipped through a gap in the hedge. Jamie and Harry watched her leave.

"I've never met a girl as bossy as her before," Harry said, wide-eyed.

Jamie laughed. "Neither have I," he agreed.

They made their way through the overgrown trees and plants back to Gnome Gardens. Jamie tried to imagine what the tangled undergrowth, gnarled old trees and derelict statues would look like in the dark. *And those creepy carvings inside the house,* he thought. A cloud blotted out the sun, plunging everything into shadow. Jamie felt himself prickle with goosebumps.

CHAPTER THREE

Hidden Twists and Turns

"Blast!" Dad said. The two wires he was holding sparked and started to smoke. "The electrics in this place have had it."

Jamie had been looking forward to playing his favourite computer game, *Creatures of Darkness III*. He and Harry stared at the tangle of wires on the living room floor, trailing to and from the TV, games console and DVD player. A chandelier hung from the high ceiling, covered in drooping cobwebs. It shone a dim light over Dad, who was sitting in the middle of the mess, looking confused. Jamie sighed.

Mum appeared in the doorway. "Looks like the swamp monsters will have to wait, boys!" she said, wiping her dusty hands on an old towel. "Why don't you explore the house instead? All those rooms to choose from!"

Jamie remembered what Milly had told them – to be careful of the Gnome. *It's just a load of rubbish*, he told himself.

"Come on," he said, dragging Harry to his feet. "Let's take a look around."

*

The wood-panelled hallway at the front of the house was carved with thorny briars and coiling branches, reminding Jamie of Milly's decorations around the well. A wide staircase, with dark wooden banisters on each side, rose up from the middle of the room.

Harry stared at a bearded wooden face peering out from the carvings. "Do you think this is the gnome Milly was on about?" he asked.

"It's like the gnome in Granddad's book," said Jamie, looking closely at its carved wooden features. "But uglier."

The face was twisted into a wicked-looking scowl. Jamie traced his fingers over the carving, feeling narrowed eyes, a sneering mouth, a deep frown and a warty nose. Suddenly, with a grinding sound, the face seemed to move. Jamie and Harry took a step back.

"What was *that*?" Harry said. He touched the face. Nothing happened.

"I think it was when I touched its nose," Jamie said, trying again.

The face moved backwards with a clunk. The wooden panel next to it slid sideways to reveal a gloomy corridor.

Jamie gasped. "Wow. A secret passage!" He felt around inside the door until he found a cord. He tugged it and a bare bulb glimmered dully, revealing crumbling plaster and cobwebs that trembled as a fat spider scuttled across them, into the shadows.

"Do you think Mum and Dad know about this?" asked Harry.

"I bet they would have told us about it," said Jamie. He coughed on the thick dust inside the passage. "It looks like no one's been inside here for years."

Jamie could see that the blood had drained from Harry's cheeks.

"Come on," Jamie said, striding ahead. "There's nothing to be scared of."

They began to walk down the narrow passageway. It twisted and turned, and Jamie noticed that his feet were leaving prints in the thick dust. Strings of cobwebs hung all around. When Jamie tried to brush them aside, they stuck to his fingers. His heart was beating hard against his chest.

"Jamie!" squawked Harry. He was pointing at a spider the size of Jamie's hand, creeping along the wall. It was so huge, Jamie could see its eyes. "How are we going to get past that?" asked Harry, trembling.

"We'll have to make a run for it," said Jamie. He grabbed Harry's hand. "Come on!"

They sprinted past the spider, ducking their heads and pushing through the cobwebs, until they reached a wooden door with coloured glass panels set into it.

Jamie looked back at his brother.

"Ready?" he asked. Harry's bottom lip was trembling but he gave a brave nod. Jamie pushed the door open to reveal a room lined with dusty bookshelves, a heavy oak desk in the middle. Stacks of papers were piled on the floor and bottles of ink stood on the desk.

"This must have been Granddad's study!"

he said. "I wonder how long it's been since anyone else came in here."

They stepped further inside. Dust covered every surface and danced in the air. The room had no windows but the walls stretched up to panes of red, green and yellow glass. A patch of green light shone on Harry, making him look like a corpse. Jamie shivered, but he forced a smile.

"You're the same colour as when you were seasick last year," he said.

The coloured light made the carvings on the walls seem even more alive than in the other rooms. Scuttling beetles appeared to lunge out of the wood, snapping their vicious-looking pincers. Grasping plant tendrils seemed about to peel away from the walls and coil around Jamie's hands.

Harry grabbed Jamie's arm and pointed to the carved snout of a snarling wolf.

Five creatures carved inside a plain oval panel stood out from the rest: a coiled snake with its head raised; a spider waving its two front legs; a swooping bat; a rat, poised as if to pounce; and a fat toad. Each had a single red jewel for an eye. The light coming through the coloured glass shifted and they glittered menacingly. It almost looked as though they were moving. . .

"They're coming for us!" yelped Harry, darting behind the desk.

CHAPTER FOUR

The Book of Gnome

"They're just carvings," said Jamie, though he felt nerves fluttering in the pit of his stomach. He gave his little brother's arm a squeeze. "Carvings can't move! Come on." He managed to persuade Harry to creep back out. The animals weren't moving at all. It had just been a trick of the light.

Jamie turned and found himself staring into a bearded face carved into the desk's middle drawer. It seemed to sneer at him. Was it the Gnome again?

This desk must have been where Granddad had done his writing. Jamie went over to the bookshelves on the wall opposite the oval panel of creatures. He scanned the spines on the old books. "*Poisonous Fungi*," he read aloud. "*Trolls and How to Thwart Them.*"

"*Cooking and Curing With Woodland Plants. Elvish for Beginners*," read Harry, looking through a pile of books on the desk. "Hey, what's this? What does it do?" he asked. Amongst the books was a black pyramid. It was the size of an orange and might have been made of glass. Its surface was pitted and dusty.

Jamie tried to pick it up but it seemed to

be stuck to the desk. "I don't know. Maybe it's a paperweight."

Next to the pyramid was the carved tip of a snake's tail. Jamie followed the tail down as it coiled around the side of the desk and down one of its legs. At the bottom of the table leg was the snake's head, its mouth open to reveal a forked tongue and sharp fangs. Jamie ran his hand over the head and felt something odd: one of its eyes seemed to be a button.

"Harry!" he said. "Come and look." Jamie suddenly had the feeling that the carved creatures in the room were drawing closer, as if they were listening. Harry knelt next to him and he pressed the button. A small drawer at the top of the desk opened with a creak. Inside it lay a book.

Carefully, Jamie took the book from the secret drawer, blew the dust from its cover and laid it on the desk.

"I've never seen a book like that before," whispered Harry.

The cover was made of worn red and green leather, the pages tipped with gold. In the middle of the front cover was a picture of a laughing gnome with a bushy white beard and sparkling eyes. He wore a red pointy hat, green trousers with red braces, and a yellow shirt – the same colours as the windowpanes. Gold letters picked out the title: *The Book of Gnome.*

"It's Granddad's book!" Harry said. "Maybe it's the original copy Mum was looking for."

"It looks like it's been there for a hundred

years," said Jamie. "Granddad wasn't *that* old!"

Together, they turned to the first yellowed page. The book's spine creaked in protest. At the top of the page was a picture of a snake. Its long green body was twisted into coils and speckled with gold leaf. The creature seemed to stare out at the boys with beady eyes, its forked tongue drawn in brilliant red ink.

Beneath the snake was a sentence. The first letter, *M*, had been beautifully drawn and brightly coloured. The rest were in a curling, old-fashioned style.

"Maybe it's the Curse of the Gnome," he said.

Harry chewed his knuckles while Jamie slowly made out each letter and read the sentence aloud: "'*My snake lives underground. . .*'"

Harry took his hand away from his mouth. "Is that it?" he said. "*That's* not scary at all!"

Jamie laughed. He stretched, feeling relief flood through him. The Curse of the Gnome was an old story; Gnome Gardens was just a run-down old house with a messy garden; and the creatures on the walls were lumps of wood. There was nothing to be scared of.

"Come on," he said to Harry. "Let's see if Dad's figured out the wiring."

Jamie shut the book and was about to return it to the drawer when a small piece of paper slipped from its pages onto the floor. He picked it up. It was a bookplate – a small piece of paper you could stick inside a book saying who it belonged to. Old glue was peeling off the back in dry yellow flakes. On the front was printed "This Book Belongs To", with something handwritten beneath it. Jamie read it to Harry:

This Book Belongs To

The Gnome of Gnome Gardens
– – – – – – – – – – – – –

Beware!
Never open my Book, unless you
want the Curse of Gnome upon you.
Or is it too late?
Then my creatures will terrify
and torment you.
You can't imagine how scared you will be.
Gnome Gardens belongs to me.
Only me. You shall see. . .

"But I thought the *Book of Gnome* was written by Granddad," said Harry, puzzled. "This says it was by the Gnome!"

"Don't be silly," said Jamie. "Granddad must have written this bookplate as some kind of joke." But he swallowed hard. The book was certainly very old; surely far older than Granddad had ever been.

Harry's voice dropped to a whisper. "When we meet Milly later . . . do you think the Gnome will be there?"

"As *if*, Harry." Jamie shoved the book back into the drawer, trying to look unconcerned. "It's just a stupid note made up to frighten people."

Harry still looked scared, his freckles standing out from his white face.

"Come on, I'll thrash you at *Creatures*," Jamie said, as he pushed Harry out of the study and into the secret passageway.

Slam! The door banged shut behind them. As Jamie turned to run after Harry, a shiver crept down his spine.

CHAPTER FIVE

The Stone Serpents

The church bells clanged dully, chiming the quarter hour: only fifteen minutes to midnight. Jamie sat on his bed, dressed and ready to go, testing the batteries in Dad's torch and wishing he hadn't made his stupid promise to Milly.

"Get a move on," he whispered to Harry.

"Can't be late and let Milly think she's scared us with her stories, can we? She'd never let us forget it."

Harry was stuffing his rucksack with a "survival kit': bottle of water, spare socks, jumper, compass. . .

"We don't need all this stuff, Harry," Jamie said. "You're not scared of a gnome, are you?"

"Course not," Harry whispered back, a tremble in his voice. "But I'm going to be ready for anything." He stuffed a packet of crisps into his bag, followed by a toy trumpet.

"OK, I *sort of* get why you're bringing a compass, and even the socks. But a *trumpet*?" Jamie reached out to grab the toy, but Harry pulled it away and shoved it firmly into the rucksack.

"Leave it, Jamie. Anything might happen. It's nearly *midnight*." Jamie didn't think this made any sense at all, but Harry was wearing one of his determined looks, so he let it go.

They tiptoed carefully out of their room and across the landing. As Jamie trod on the first stair, it creaked loudly. They both froze: would Mum and Dad wake up? Jamie stared at their parents' closed bedroom door, until the rumble of Dad's loud snore made him turn to Harry with a grin. Jamie put a finger to his lips. They crept down the dark staircase, past looming, unfamiliar shapes. Jamie unlocked the back door, and they were out into the night.

The moonlight cast sinister shadows across the garden. Jamie noticed the lightning tree he'd spotted during the day, its dead branches pointing into the night. He thought they looked just like bony fingers.

Harry let out a small yelp. "What's that, over there?"

Jamie switched on his torch. A dark shape swooped through its beam of light.

"Just an owl," said Jamie, laughing nervously as they set off towards the well. The wind shook the trees with a ghostly, shivering *swisshhh*, and something slunk out of the bushes.

"What's that?" hissed Harry, clutching Jamie's arm.

Jamie waved the torch, picking out a fox's pointed ears and bushy tail.

"Argh!" he shouted as something whirred by his face, and he swatted the air furiously – until he saw it was just a moth.

They spotted Milly before she saw them. Her shoulders were hunched and she had wrapped her arms around her body as if she were freezing cold, despite the warm night air. They made their way towards her, the long grass rustling.

"Who's there?" Milly cried out, spinning round. But when she saw Jamie and Harry she relaxed and leaned against the side of the well, as though she visited overgrown gardens at midnight every night of the week.

"What kept you?" she asked. "I'd almost given up waiting." She gave a pretend yawn.

"Did you hear that yelping noise?"

"Yes," said Harry, "that was Ja—"

"Must have been a fox," said Jamie quickly.

Milly peered in the direction of the church tower. Its white clock face glowed against the purple sky like a second moon. "Two minutes to midnight," she said.

"Nothing's going to happen," Jamie insisted.

"Of course it won't," said Milly. "Not after the effort I went to with the well. I just want to see if you two have the guts to stay out here at midnight."

"Course we do," said Jamie. He leaned against the side of the well too.

They waited in silence.

Harry stared up at the church clock. "I wonder how the hands go round," he murmured. Milly did her bored yawning routine again. Jamie ran his fingers over the stone snakes coiled round the well, imagining how much their bite would hurt if they were real. His mouth was dry and his stomach was tied in knots. *What am I getting so worried about?* He switched the torch on and off a few times, pulled a monster face and staggered about like a zombie. They all laughed nervously.

Bonnnggg. . .

The night air split with the first chime of midnight.

Bonnnggg. . .

The three of them stood still, looking at one another and listening to the echoing clangs.

Bonnnggg. . .

The twelfth chime faded away.

Still nothing had happened.

Jamie felt relief wash over him. He began

to laugh. "Ancient curses, monsters, evil gnomes — it's all a load of rubbish! Come on, let's—"

The sound of slithering made his words dry up in his throat. Harry was tugging at Jamie's sleeve, pointing wordlessly at the well. Milly gasped and backed away. Slowly, Jamie turned round — and felt the blood drain from his face.

On the rim of the well, the stone snakes were moving — uncoiling, peeling away from the stone and slithering down the side of the well. They were alive!

CHAPTER SIX

Into the Well

"It's the Curse of Gnome!" screamed Milly.

Forked tongues flickered between stone fangs and bright beady eyes peered out of dull rock. Then the stone changed to shining scales as the snakes squirmed and slithered down the side of the well. They hissed horribly, the pale light of the moon shining off their bodies. More of the creatures emerged from inside the well to slide across the grass, their pointed tongues tasting the air.

"Let's get out of here," Jamie yelled. "Run!" He heard a cry. Swivelling round, he saw. . .

"Harry!" Two long brown snakes were wrapped around his brother's ankles, hissing and spitting. Harry's eyes were wide with fear, and he gave a yell as the snakes yanked his legs so that he fell to the ground with a jolt.

Jamie grabbed his arm. "It's all right, I've got you!" he shouted, trying to pull Harry out of the snakes' grasp.

Milly seized Harry's other arm and

pulled too, but the snakes' powerful bodies tightened their grip. Others joined them and they began dragging him towards the well. Harry kicked his legs and squirmed, clinging to Jamie and Milly's arms. The snakes held fast.

"Get them off me!" he shouted.

"We will!" yelled Jamie. He yanked at Harry's arms, pulling as hard as he could – but he couldn't stop his brother from slipping backwards. The snakes hissed more loudly. *No!* Jamie thought. *I can't let this happen. . .*

Milly let go of Harry's arm, grabbed a branch from her display and used it to try to prise the snakes from his legs. Their heads darted round and they bared their fangs, but didn't loosen their grip.

Harry's free hand grabbed a tree root, his knuckles white as he clung on. Milly tried to uncoil the snakes.

"Get off!" she panted.

Jamie felt his grip begin to slip as more snakes entwined themselves around Harry, pulling him away. "No!" he yelled.

But Harry was wrenched out of Jamie's grasp and dragged up the stone wall of the well, his hands clawing at the air, terror in his eyes. More snakes coiled around his waist and, with a sudden jerk, he disappeared down the well shaft.

"*Jamie!*" Harry's frightened voice echoed upwards.

Milly and Jamie looked at one another, then at the well. "Come on!" they said together.

They scrambled over the side, clinging to the rusty chain suspended above the blackness.

Jamie went down first, climbing hand over hand. "Harry!" he yelled. But there was no answer.

His torch started to slip from his pocket, and when he lunged for it he lost his grip and plunged down the well shaft, splashing into the black water. The bucket bashed him in the face.

"Are you OK?" shouted Milly, from where she still clung to the chain.

"I'm fine." Jamie was treading water, looking around the well. At least he had managed to keep hold of the torch. "Harry!" he called again. But there was still no reply, just the sound of dripping and a constant ssing. Where had his brother disappeared to? Jamie felt thick reeds wrap around his legs. He tried to kick them away, but one of the reeds squirmed and scales brushed against his skin.

"Watch out!" he warned Milly. "There're more snakes in the water."

Milly carefully lowered herself down next to him. "I can feel them wriggling about – it's horrible!"

Jamie shone the torch around, lighting the cold, black well water, the glistening scales of the snakes – and Milly's pale face and thick hair. She was thrashing about to stay afloat. Then her eyes suddenly widened and she vanished beneath the surface of the snake-filled water.

Jamie splashed towards the place she'd

disappeared, feeling for her under the water. He couldn't lose her too! He felt an arm and pulled. Milly broke the surface with a splash, shaking her head and coughing, slime streaking her face. Jamie untangled a wriggling snake from her hair and threw it to the other side of the well.

"Urgh!" Milly spluttered. "We have to get out of here!"

"Harry!" Jamie yelled, as loudly as he could. Milly joined in. But there was no answering shout. Jamie couldn't bear to think about what might be happening to his brother. How were they going to find him?

"Jamie! Over there," said Milly, pointing and gasping for breath.

Jamie shone his torch at the wall and

saw that on one of the bricks was a snarling face with a pointy hat and bushy beard. The Gnome. Maybe this gnome's face opened a door, like the one in the house? He splashed frantically towards it, shaking off a thick snake that slithered across his arm.

He reached up and pushed the gnome carving as hard as he could. At first, nothing happened. Jamie felt a wave of panic, then remembered the nose. He pressed there. It worked! The brick slid backwards. With a loud grinding noise, part of the wall moved sideways to reveal a passageway above their heads.

"I'll go first," said Milly. She grabbed the ledge and heaved herself into it, then helped Jamie clamber up. His knees and elbows scraped against the rough brick. Soon the two of them were standing in the dank, narrow passage.

"You OK?" asked Jamie.

Milly nodded. She was dripping wet, shivering, and her face was smeared with slime. "*Now* do you believe me about the Curse?" she asked.

Jamie nodded. "Let's go."

They squeezed through a narrow gap, which opened into a rocky tunnel. Angry hisses filled the damp air and Jamie's torchlight picked out reptiles dangling from the ceiling, like the tendrils of some horrible plant. More snakes slithered up the walls and writhed beneath their feet.

"They're everywhere!" shrieked Milly, pulling away a snake that was wriggling through her hair.

Jamie gritted his teeth. "Come on," he said, "let's run!"

They sprinted through the tunnel, their feet sliding over the snakes. Light shone at the end of the tunnel, and Jamie switched the torch off, saving the battery. He slipped it into his pocket. *Who knows how long we're going to be stuck down here?* Now, as he ran past, he could see all the snakes clearly. Most of them were long and brown with a red, yellow and green diamond on their heads, but there were other kinds too. A rattlesnake shook its tail, and Milly jumped away from a hooded cobra that swayed in the shadows. Jamie felt his stomach churn.

The tunnel rounded a corner, and he and Milly emerged into a huge, brightly lit cavern. Glittering stalagmites – pillars of

rock slowly growing towards the ceiling –
stretched up among the mass of snakes that
covered the floor. Instead of writhing, they
were deathly still, and staring at something
as if hypnotized. Jamie followed their gaze to
a small patch of ground. There sat Harry, his
knees drawn up to his face. The thousands of
beady, reptilian eyes were watching him.

Jamie cupped his hands together and
yelled, "Harry! Don't worry, we're here!"
But his heart lurched. How was he going
to rescue his brother?

CHAPTER SEVEN

The Cavern of Serpents

Harry looked up. "Jamie! Milly!"

The snakes' heads darted round and they slithered across the rocky ground towards the children. They reared up, hissing and baring their fangs, giving threatening rattles. Jamie and Milly were surrounded. Jamie felt his hands turn clammy. There was only one escape route: back down the passageway. *And we've only just found Harry*, Jamie thought. *I'm not losing him again.*

A rattlesnake lunged towards Jamie. He ducked out of the way, but his foot caught on a rock and he sprawled in the dirt. *Hisssss.* A red and black cobra loomed over him, its hood raised, coiled and ready to strike.

"Leave him alone!" yelled Harry, leaping to his feet. Jamie saw him try to move across the cavern, but a circle of snakes hemmed him in.

The cobra was snaking closer towards Jamie. Then suddenly – *wham*! Milly kicked the cobra into the shadows, her trainer whistling past Jamie's nose. "Got it!" she said.

"Milly, watch out," said Jamie as he scrambled up, pointing at Milly's feet.

His friend glanced down. Some of the bigger snakes had coiled themselves around her ankles. "Get off me!" she cried, trying to kick them away.

Before he could move to help her, more snakes slithered up Jamie's body. He kicked and struggled, but their coils strapped his arms tightly to his body. Milly thrashed and yelled as the snakes dragged her to where Harry stood. And all the time, the snakes' coils tightened around Jamie, pinching his skin like scaly hands. The snakes heaved to one side and he was pulled off his feet and hauled along the ground, his head bumping the floor. Finally, he arrived next to Harry and Milly in the centre of the cavern.

The snakes formed a circle around the three of them, Jamie and Milly huddled close together with Harry in the middle. Every so often, one of the snakes darted forward, eyes blank and forked tongue flickering, as if ready to strike. Jamie, Harry and Milly spun around, dizzyingly, trying to keep clear of the snakes' flashing fangs.

"Look out!" yelled Jamie, yanking Milly and Harry backwards to dodge a lunging cobra. As he spun them round, Jamie's elbow struck something hard.

"Harry – your survival kit!" he gasped. "Quick. . ."

Harry slipped his backpack off and Jamie fumbled with the zip. He wrenched it open and rummaged through the contents.

"There must be something here that will help us."

Milly pushed aside the socks and compass and pulled out the bottle of water. "Yes!" she said triumphantly. "Snakes usually live in deserts, so the water should scare them away." She tipped some into her hand and threw it at the snakes in front of them. But instead of being frightened, they hissed angrily and drew even closer. Jamie, Harry and Milly were caught in a tight circle, their backs together, and nowhere to go.

It's hopeless, thought Jamie. *We've nothing to defend ourselves with.* He dropped the backpack to the ground – and something hard inside it struck his foot. He tried to imagine what it could be. . .

"The trumpet!" he cried, pulling it out.

He ducked as a snake lunged at him. "I've seen snake charmers on TV. They play a tune, and the snake goes into a trance!"

"Quick!" Harry cried, holding out his open palm.

As Jamie and Milly did their best to kick the snakes aside, Harry brought the toy trumpet to his lips and blew hard. It made a raspberry sound. He tried again, and this time there was a strangled squeak. The snakes opened their jaws wide and reared up, ready to sink their fangs into Jamie, Harry and Milly.

A blood-chilling howl cut through the air. A tiny, bent old man stepped out from behind a stalagmite. A pair of snakes hissed wickedly from the pocket of his filthy yellow shirt. Thin wisps of hair sprouted from his chin and escaped from his greasy red cap. His wrinkled face was contorted with rage, and as he snarled he revealed yellow, pointed teeth.

Jamie's voice was thick with fear. "The Gnome!"

CHAPTER EIGHT

The Transformation

"Stupid children," said the Gnome, his yellow teeth bared. His cruel eyes flickered across their faces. "*Very* stupid children. I did warn you. Didn't you see my little note?"

"He's real," whimpered Harry, holding onto Jamie's arm. "He's going to get us!"

The Gnome stepped towards them, his ugly face twisted into a mocking grin. "I told you my creatures would terrify you. This house belongs only to me – me! You shouldn't be here at all. None of you! Prepare to be scared out of your minds by my pretty snakes." His cackle echoed round the cavern.

The snakes. . . Jamie saw that they were watching the Gnome, their heads swivelled towards him. Now was their chance!

"Run!" Jamie cried. They bolted for the passageway. But the snakes surged forward to block the entrance, forming a thick, wriggling column.

Harry gripped Jamie's arm, his face white with fear. "Look – the snakes are joining up!"

Jamie stared. As the snakes wound across one another, their coils fused together. Flickering tongues grew and turned into red scales, and beady eyes became part of a pattern of dots. Soon all the snakes in the cavern had merged to become one gigantic, massively powerful serpent, glistening with red, green and yellow scales. *Hissssss*. It towered above them, its open jaws revealing dripping fangs.

"How does it do that?" Harry managed to ask, despite the tremble in his voice.

Jamie's heart pounded. It was the snake from *The Book of Gnome*. They would never escape from *this*.

"It's playtime," said the Gnome, stroking the serpent's scales with his gnarled hand. "Get rid of these children!"

The creature thrust its huge head at them, jaws open wide, then drew back, flexing its coils. A drop of green venom splattered onto Jamie's arm and burned the skin, making him cry out. But he swallowed his fear. He wasn't going to be beaten by the Gnome – at least, not without a fight.

"You can't hurt us!" he shouted. "You're not even real. You're just a stupid story!"

The Gnome gave a short, ugly laugh. "Not real? Why don't you come here, then?" He beckoned to Jamie with a curled, bony finger.

Jamie shook his head. He looked around the glittering cavern, into the eyes of the terrifying giant snake. He felt the rock beneath his feet and smelled the damp air. Beside him, Harry was shaking and Milly's face was pinched and bloodless. It was real. It was very real.

The Gnome gave a snort of laughter. "This house has been mine for hundreds of years. First I had to put up with that foolish old man, and now you three." He spat on the floor. "Well, it won't be for long."

"You won't get away with this!" cried Jamie bravely, his arms around Harry and Milly. He felt his legs wobble.

"Why, what are you going to do? Tell your dear departed *granddad*?"

Harry looked up at Jamie. "Do y-y-you think h-h-he hurt Granddad?" he stammered.

Jamie felt a rush of hot anger flood through him. "We're stronger than you," he said to the Gnome, "and we're going to get out of here."

"You really think so?" said the Gnome, folding his arms. "You're even more stupid than you look." He bared his teeth at them again, and snarled, "I'm having my house back *now*."

The monstrous snake lunged across the ground. It gave a rasping hiss and, lightning-fast, wrapped its body around the three of them. Jamie felt the air being pushed out of his lungs. He, Harry and Milly pushed at the snake's rippling scales, but that only seemed to make it squeeze harder.

The Gnome's cruel laughter bounced off the cavern walls. "It's over!" he cackled. "I'll enjoy watching my creature eat your flesh and pick your bones."

Jamie could see great muscles rippling underneath the snake's scales, gripping tighter and tighter, making him fight for breath.

"Harry," gasped Milly in a strangled voice. "Try the trumpet again!"

Harry was still clutching the toy. His arms were crushed against his chest, but he managed to put it to his lips. Again, only a pathetic, squeaky note came out.

Jamie shuddered – he could see right down the giant snake's gaping throat, feel the damp touch of its sour breath as it brought its jaws closer to them. *Its jaws. . .* Jamie stared from them to Harry's trumpet, then at the serpent again. It seemed impossible. But what other chance did they have?

"That's it!" Jamie shouted. He grabbed the trumpet from Harry.

"What are you doing?" Milly asked.

"I'm going to jam the snake's jaws with the trumpet!"

The creature's head loomed above them. It hissed, then opened its mouth wide, showing fangs as long as carving knives. Its eyes narrowed and it lunged down at Jamie, ready to swallow him. "No!" yelled Harry and Milly.

Jamie thrust the trumpet up towards the snake's gaping mouth. But just as Jamie felt its hot, rancid breath, the snake snapped its head away again, drawing high amongst the shadowy stalactites.

"There's no escape," said the Gnome, but Jamie thought he saw a flash of worry cross his ugly face.

Then, to Jamie's amazement, Harry spoke

in a strong, steady voice. "We'll have to hold its head."

"Yes," agreed Milly. "Me and Harry each grab a fang. You stick the trumpet in its throat."

The snake's jaws were open again, ready for another strike. Quick as a cracking whip, it lunged, two vicious, yellow fangs descending on them fast.

Harry and Milly each grabbed a fang, wincing as the venom burned their skin. Jamie could see their arms trembling as they struggled to keep the snake's jaws held in place. He quickly thrust the trumpet between the snake's fangs. "That's it!" he cried, feeling the trumpet lodge inside the creature's mouth.

Their plan had worked!

CHAPTER NINE

A New Discovery

Harry and Milly let go and the serpent recoiled, shaking its head from side to side. It rasped out a horrible, gurgling hiss.

"No!" shrieked the Gnome, his eyes narrowed into slits. His bent, bony frame seemed to pulse with fury.

As the snake thrashed its head, Jamie felt

its coils begin to loosen. He pushed as hard as he could against the cold scales.

"It's stopped squeezing us," said Milly, as she and Harry pushed too.

Jamie drew in a big lungful of air, able to breathe freely at last.

The three of them clambered over the snake's coils, ducking to avoid its thrashing head.

The Gnome jabbed a long, filthy fingernail at Jamie. "You'll regret this," he hissed through his sharp teeth. "I'll finish you off myself." He marched towards them, his narrow eyes glittering, forcing Jamie, Harry and Milly to back away.

But the serpent was still writhing on the ground, coiling and uncoiling its vast body. Its tail whipped round as it tossed about, knocking the Gnome against a stalagmite. The rock crumbled apart, and with a cry of fury, the Gnome was buried under a pile of stones. Jamie could just see a flash of his red cap and a bony hand poking through the rubble. The hand wasn't moving.

"Is he dead?" asked Harry quietly.

Jamie slowly stepped towards the pile of rubble. He knelt down beside it, but the rocks and the Gnome beneath them were perfectly still. He turned and smiled at Harry and Milly.

"We've done it—" he began. But the Gnome's hand shot out and grabbed his wrist.

Jamie gave a yell, snapping his arm free.

"This isn't over," the Gnome snarled. His hideous face appeared as he struggled free from the rubble. He lobbed a fist-sized stone at them, which smashed by Milly's feet. "You can't escape the Curse!"

Jamie grabbed the other two. "Come on," he shouted. "Let's go!"

They ran to the tunnel. Jamie took out the torch and pressed it into Harry's hand, pushing Milly and Harry in front of him as they entered the dark, narrow passage. About halfway along, he heard scratching and panting in the darkness behind them. "The Gnome's following us!" he warned.

"I've got an idea," Milly shouted. "Keep going!"

Stumbling over the rocks and bumping into each other, they squeezed through the narrow gap. "Quick!" said Milly. "Fill it up with stones!"

They frantically gathered stones from the passage, and piled them up in the gap. Harry's torch flashed over their tired faces as he held it between his teeth. When the gap was plugged, Jamie and Harry rolled a big rock in front of it. *I just hope it gives us enough time to escape*, thought Jamie.

They sprinted along the passage and reached the doorway to the well.

"One. Two. Three!" Harry chanted. Then the three of them leapt down into the water.

Jamie struggled through the stagnant water to the chain. "I'll climb to the top and wind you two up in the bucket." He put a hand on the chain, then turned to Harry and Milly. Their faces looked dead white in the torchlight. "We'll soon be home," he said.

Jamie inched up the slippery chain, exhausted, the rusty metal biting painfully into his hands. He reached the top and heaved himself over the rim of the well. "OK!" he called down.

He felt someone's weight in the bucket below. "Ready to go," called Harry.

Using all his strength, Jamie turned the old iron handle that winched up the bucket. It felt as though it hadn't been used in a very long time and creaked in protest. Harry scrambled out. Together, he and Jamie hurriedly turned the handle to let the bucket down again. They heard it splash.

Milly's voice echoed up from below. "Hurry up, you two – I can hear the Gnome moving the stones!"

Jamie and Harry turned the handle

together as fast as they could. The bucket swung against the side of the shaft as they heaved, and soon Jamie could see Milly's outline. "Just a few more turns," shouted Jamie.

But, just as Milly was almost at the top, there was a clunk and the bucket lurched downward.

"One of the chain links has worn through!" Milly cried, her voice echoing from inside the well.

Jamie could see that Milly was suspended by a single rusty piece of metal. "Aarggh!" she shouted, scrambling frantically up the chain, the torch tumbling into the water and fizzling out.

"Milly! Jump!" Jamie cried. He and Harry leaned into the well, their hands stretched out towards him. Jamie could hear faint cries carrying up from the angry Gnome.

The chain link bent slowly open and with a sudden, brittle snap, it broke completely. Milly threw herself at Jamie and Harry, and as they caught her the chain clattered down into the water below.

"Don't let go!" Milly begged, tears streaking her face.

"Pull!" Jamie cried.

He and Harry hauled Milly over the edge of the well, where they collapsed in a heap on the damp grass. They looked at one another, still panting. Milly's long hair was plastered against her head. All of them were wet and filthy. It looked as though Harry was getting a black eye.

"Let's check," said Milly, wiping her eyes

and slowly getting to her feet. "Make sure there's nothing coming after us."

They peered down the well. In the moonlight they could just make out the bucket floating in the water. The sides of the well looked solid, with no passageway breaking up the brickwork – though Milly had jumped from it only moments before. No snakes, no angry cries and no Gnome. It was just an old well with a broken chain.

Jamie felt his heart-rate slowing down to normal. He leaned against the rim of the well, his head bowed in relief. The stone felt smooth. . .

"Harry, Milly," he said quietly, taking a step back, "look at the edge of the well."

Instead of the horrible snake carvings,

the rim of the well was covered in stone flowers – honeysuckle, roses and poppies.

"That proves it," said Milly, "we did it! We defeated the Gnome and the Curse is lifted!" She grabbed Jamie and Harry by the hand and began a little dance of triumph.

Jamie and Harry pulled themselves free and looked at each other uneasily.

"Milly," said Jamie. "There's something we need to tell you."

"What?" Milly's smile faded as she stopped dancing. "The snakes have gone and everything's OK now. Isn't it?"

"We found a creepy old book," Harry began, "called *The Book of Gnome*. We thought our granddad wrote it, but inside there was an old bookplate saying it was written by the Gnome. His creatures are going to keep attacking us – until he gets Gnome Gardens back."

"You mean. . ." Milly looked up at the huge house that towered over them. A bat fluttered out from the eaves.

"That's right," said Harry. "There are more creepy creatures."

Jamie, Harry and Milly crept through the secret passage into the study. The first rays of early morning sunlight shone through the coloured glass of the ceiling. It caught on the jewelled eyes of the five creatures in the oval panel.

"Look!" gasped Harry. He was pointing at the snake carving.

Jamie realized that the snake's head was moving. It was no trick of the light this time. It turned to face into the room, its two red eyes glinting.

"I knew there was something scary about those carvings," whispered Harry.

Milly turned to *The Book of Gnome* on the desk. She took a deep breath. "Let's find out what creatures we're going to meet next."

Jamie opened the book to the picture of the snake, and they all three held the edge of the yellowed, brittle page. Jamie glanced at Harry and Milly's faces. They were streaked yellow, red and green by the light shining through the stained glass. The Gnome's colours.

"Ready?" Jamie whispered.

They turned the page.

Milly gave a gasp.

Fear crawled down Jamie's spine, like eight

scuttling, hairy legs. There was a carefully drawn picture of a huge spider, its eyes picked out in scarlet ink and each gruesome hair on its body ending in a gold tip. Teeth like daggers lined its mouth. Beneath the drawing was a sentence. "*Beware the spider's embrace,*" Jamie read out.

"I *hate* spiders," said Harry, his voice trembling.

They slammed the book shut and a cloud of dust billowed up into their faces. Jamie swallowed hard.

"Listen," he told the others, as they crept back out into the secret corridor. The study door swung shut heavily behind them. "We're going to have to be very careful. The Curse of the Gnome is real. Who knows what's going to happen next?"

Join Jamie, Harry and Milly in the
next **CREEPY CREATURES** adventure!

Turn the page for a sneak preview . . .

CHAPTER ONE

Shifting Shadows

What's that!

Jamie walked into the ancient nursery
in Gnome Gardens. He saw a dark shape
scuttle through the shadows. His hand
shaking, he flicked on the light switch –
but the shape disappeared. The room was
perfectly still. The only movement came

from the ivy blowing in the wind outside, tapping at the windows like ghostly fingers.

Jamie shook himself.

Two pairs of footsteps echoed up the stairs.

"Hurry up!" called Jamie. "I've found the perfect room for our midnight feast." He wouldn't tell the others about whatever it was he'd spotted in the dark – no point in ruining the evening's adventure.

"We're coming!" Jamie's brother, Harry, shouted back.

"*You* try hauling this stuff up two flights of stairs!" Milly called. Jamie and Harry had met Milly, their next-door neighbour, when they'd moved in.

The old nursery was a huge, dusty room

at the top of the house. By the fireplace, a rocking horse with a bedraggled mane and tail stared at the floor with dull painted eyes. An ancient chest of drawers leaned against one wall, and next to it was a dolls' house, nearly as tall as Jamie. The dolls' house reminded Jamie of Gnome Gardens – grey, sprawling and run-down, with turrets and gargoyles, like a picture of a haunted house in a book.

Jamie and Harry had arrived at Gnome Gardens a few weeks ago. The house used to belong to their granddad, who'd spent years alone here writing his books, including his famous *Book of Gnome*. Jamie and Harry had been fed up with hearing about it – until they found the original copy of *The Book of Gnome*. That ancient book held a terrifying secret. An evil Gnome had put a curse on this house!

Harry appeared in the doorway with Milly. They were both wearing pyjamas, just like Jamie. Harry's had cartoon trains all over them. Milly's pyjamas had grey-and-white stripes – she didn't like anything fussy – and her hair was in two long plaits. They peered at Jamie from behind the pile of sheets, sleeping bags, duvets and pillows they were carrying, then dumped everything on the floor and looked around. Milly brushed the hair out of her face, her cheeks glowing.

"That thing's creepy," said Harry, pointing at the dolls' house.

"No, it's not," said Milly, picking up a sheet and shaking it out. "It's only an old toy. We can use it to make a tent."

She draped the sheet between the dolls' house roof and the chest of drawers, tucking a corner into one of the drawers. She used another sheet to make a flap for the entrance, tucking that into a drawer too. Finally, she opened the flap and sat inside her tent, looking pleased with herself.

"That's brilliant," Jamie said, impressed.

"And look, I brought this." Milly unrolled a sleeping bag and took out something that looked like a rocket. She plugged it into a socket by the dolls' house. The rocket lit up, casting a green glow inside the tent, then yellow, then red. Inside it, globules of liquid rose to the top, forming swirling shapes. The shapes cast strange shadows before they slowly sank to the bottom again.

"What's that?" Harry asked. "How does it work?"

"It's called a lava lamp," Milly said proudly. "It's got wax in it, which gets heated up and moves."

Harry went to examine it more closely. "It's making weird shapes on the walls," he said.

Jamie thought one of the shadows looked like a giant, swaying snake. He ducked inside the tent and started arranging sleeping bags, duvets and pillows. "Come on, Harry."

His brother crawled in, carrying a duvet. He was wearing the same backpack he took everywhere.

"What's in your survival kit this time?" Jamie asked, smiling. "I knew you'd bring it along. After all, everyone knows midnight feasts are *really* dangerous."

"You never know. Not in this house," said Harry. He brought out a bag of crisps, a pair of Dad's gardening gloves, a small plastic bucket and spade, still covered in sand from their last trip to the beach, and a net bag of shiny gold chocolate coins. Then he turned the backpack upside down and shook it. "That's funny," he said, frowning. "I'm sure I put my silver car in here."

"Your favourite one?" Jamie asked.

Harry nodded.

"It'll turn up. Anyway, I'm glad you brought the crisps and chocolate. If Mum's mountain of snacks runs out, they'll be our emergency supplies!"

"What emergency?" asked Harry in a small voice. Jamie rolled his eyes.

"You can tease now," Milly said, "but you weren't laughing the last time we needed Harry's survival kit. We'd never have got away from the Gnome and his snakes without his toy trumpet."

The three of them fell silent. Jamie shivered as he remembered being attacked by a mass of writhing, hissing snakes, wrapping their coils around his arms and legs. But even the snakes hadn't been as terrifying as their master, the evil Gnome.

"Did you tell your parents about what happened?" asked Milly.

Jamie shook his head. "They'd never believe it. *I* wouldn't believe it if I hadn't been there."

"My mum thought my clothes were filthy from playing by the river," said Milly. "She—"

A yelp from Harry interrupted her.

"What's that?" Harry was pointing through the tent flap towards the dolls' house. Something was moving inside one of the bottom windows.

I was right, thought Jamie. *There* is *something in the nursery. . .*

A long, hairy leg reached through the window, feeling for the floor. Another leg poked out, and another. An enormous, hairy spider, as big as Jamie's hand, struggled out and squatted on a dusty floorboard.

"Urgh!" Harry shrank back.

Jamie remembered the words in the *Book of Gnome* about the next creature they would meet: *Beware the spider's embrace*. Had this spider been sent by the Gnome? Jamie grabbed the plastic spade and tapped it sharply on the floorboard in front of the creature. It scuttled towards the wall and squeezed underneath a gap in the skirting board.

Harry shuddered and moved back further into the tent. He patted his backpack. "See?" he said. "My survival kit saved us again!"

"Shhhh!" Milly put her finger to her lips. "Listen."

The stairs creaked, one by one. Someone was climbing them, slowly.

Creak.

"It's the Gnome!" said Harry desperately.

They looked at one another. There was a pause.

Creak.

The footsteps were moving across the landing, towards the nursery. In the crack of light under the door, Jamie could see the shadowy outline of two feet. His heart pounded as he heard fingers scrabbling at the door handle. He grabbed the plastic spade, holding it before him like a sword as the handle began to turn. . .

Look out for. . .

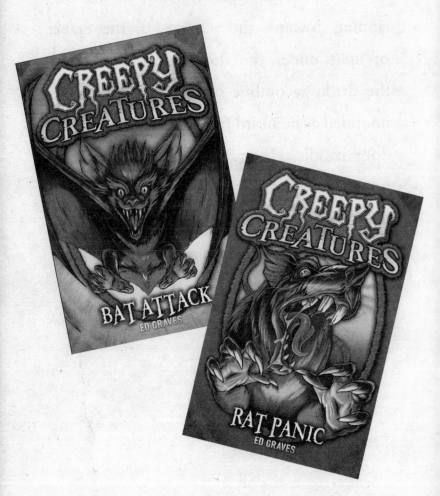